# MY TWO COOL MOMS

### Kristine Ebona

Ordering Information:
Quantity sales. Special discounts are available on quantity purchases by
corporations, associations, and others. For details, contact the publisher at
kristineebona@gmail.com or visit www.extragaysians.com.

**ISBN:** 9798586676832

Always choose kindness.

To my grandmother Enriqueta,
who was a remarkable and beautiful soul.

She was a wonderful combination
of endless and magnificent stories,
comfort and kindness,
laughter and unconditional love.

I live my life as her legacy.

# MY TWO COOL MOMS

by Kristine Ebona

We were talking about families in school.
Ms. Mary asked, "What makes your family unique?"

Nahid quickly raised her hand at the same time as mine.

Since ladies always go first, I put my arm down and I looked at her.

"My mom is the best because she makes delicious lunches like chicken kabob!" Nahid said.

"Every Sunday, my dad takes me to Persian school to learn Farsi then we go for ice cream," she added.

"My grandma always takes me for ice cream on Sundays too!" Sidney responded. "Because I live with her, most people think she is my mother."

"Grandma Enriqueta is both my mom and my dad." Sidney said softly. A few of the kids laughed at her.

I felt scared. I did not want to share about my family anymore.

My family is not like everybody else's — my family is different.

"Now kids!" Ms. Mary interrupted the laughs and the giggles.

"All families are different and unique," Ms. Mary said.

"Some families are also created in different ways, but they all have one thing in common which is love."

I felt really brave, I raised my hand right away!

"I have two cool moms!"

"Last year, my moms took me to visit Canada!"

"Riding the airplane and visiting my grandma Nel is my favorite part."

"Also, every Saturday, my mom Gloria plays basketball with me."

"She has the best jump shot!"

"My mom Kristine made me a ninja costume this Halloween!"

"Next year she will teach me Muay Thai."

"A Mai Tai! My mom loves those!" Mikassa added.

"Muay Thai is like having ninja skills," I said.

"Whoa cool Ninja skills!" Caden said loudly.

"I have two dads!" Shane shouted.

"One is bald and one is hairy."

"But they both make the best peanut butter sandwiches." Everyone laughed.

"Every family is different, not one is the same."

"My family is unique."
"It is not like everyone else's or yours."

"But there's nobody else I'd rather have for my parents than my Two Cool Moms."

# ABOUT THE AUTHOR

Kristine Ebona is the author of *My Two Cool Moms*. She is passionate about everything LGBTQ+ advocacy-related, Muay Thai, archiving food pictures on Instagram, and a questionable Twitch DJ career.

After 11 dull years of working in the Oil and Gas industry, she returned to school to pursue Marketing — a designation that provided her with high-key phenomenal story-telling skills and another set of devastating student loans.

She is also the founder of Tata X Digital Agency where she guides clients to elevate their marketing efforts beyond sticking flyers on vehicle windshields.

When the pandemic hit in 2020, instead of annoying her wife — she decided to channel her creative outlet in a pragmatic way. She set out on a mission to write books that empowers children in modern families. She believes in the importance of diversity in children's books because each child deserves to see themselves in art.

Kristine's websites are *extragaysians.com*, *tatax.team*, and can be found on Instagram *@Extragaysians*.

Made in the USA
Middletown, DE
30 September 2023

39839211R00020